Stepping Through Time

Contents

Kerri Lane

Rigby

Introduction

Shoes are like jackets for our feet!

We wear shoes:

- to keep our feet warm or cool

- to protect our feet from the rough ground

- to help us play games and sports

Shoes can show us what people and places were like. In this book, you will step through time and see the sorts of shoes people wore long ago.

The First Shoes

Early humans wrapped animal skins around their feet and tied them at the ankle. The skins protected their feet from the rough ground.

These shoes looked more like bags than like the shoes we wear today.

Ancient Sandals

The ancient Egyptians lived in a very hot land. They wore sandals to keep their feet cool and to protect their feet from the hot sand.

Most Egyptians wore sandals made from palm leaves. Sometimes they painted pictures on the soles of their sandals.

These sandals had long, pointed toes. Egyptian kings wore them. This showed ordinary people how important the kings were.

The ancient Romans and Greeks also lived in a hot land. Like the Egyptians, they wore sandals, too. Their sandals were made of leather.

Roman soldiers wore sandals that laced high up their legs. This showed that they were very important people.

The ancient Greeks liked playing sports and games. They often wore sandals that helped support their feet and ankles.

Traditional Shoes

Native Americans improved on the idea of wrapping animal skins around feet.

They made shoes to fit their feet. These shoes were called *moccasins*.

Moccasins were made from animal hides such as deer or buffalo. They had soft soles that helped hunters walk quietly when searching for food.

These are the traditional shoes of Japan. They are called *geta*.

The "stilts" on the bottom keep the wearer's feet above the wet ground.

Look at these colorful traditional boots. Mongolian horsemen wear them during the cold winter.

7

Weird and Wonderful Shoes

In Europe, hundreds and hundreds of years ago, shoes were made in many different shapes, colors, and styles.

Look at the shapes of these shoes!

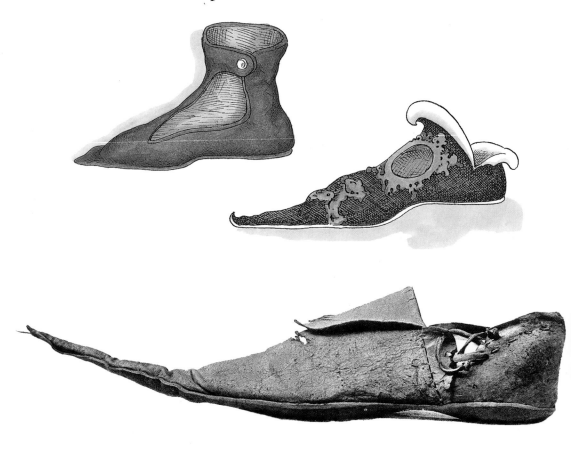

People wore shoes that had very long toes. These shoes were called *crackowes*. The long toes were sometimes stuffed with hair or moss.

The men in this very old painting are wearing crackowes.

Some people wore only stockings to protect their feet. When it was wet, shoes like these were worn to keep the stockings dry.

People also wore boots made from leather. Some leather boots were made with whalebone. The whale bone helped stiffen the pointy toes.

These shoes were very common. Their style was based on the ancient Greek sandals.

Look at this shoe! It's called a "bear's paw" and was made in Germany.

Fancy Shoes

As time went by, shoes became very stylish. They were made out of many different materials and came in many fancy styles.

In Venice, some ladies wore shoes like these, called *chopines*.

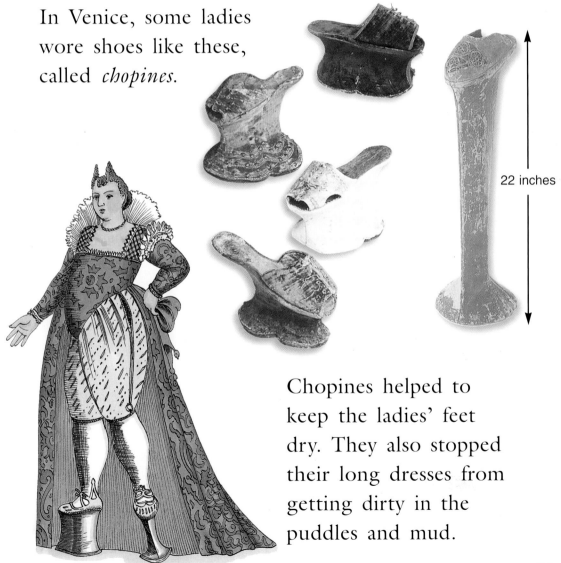

22 inches

Chopines helped to keep the ladies' feet dry. They also stopped their long dresses from getting dirty in the puddles and mud.

11

Some women wore shoes called *pattens*. These "overshoes" protected another pair of shoes from the dirty streets. They were very hard to walk in!

Some men wore lace to decorate their boots. The tops of their boots were wide, like buckets.

Men also wore fancy shoes. King Louis XIV of France wore shoes with heels. He wanted to show that he was "higher" than everybody else.

Boots Made for Walking

As time passed, boots were very popular with both men and women.

These ladies' traveling boots were worn for walking or traveling.

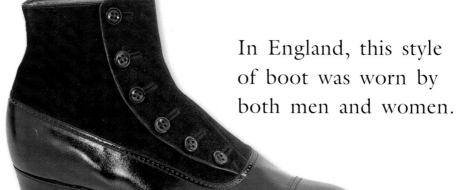

In England, this style of boot was worn by both men and women.

Look at these boots. They were very modern for their time. They had elastic sides and were easy to put on.

Beautiful slippers were also popular with men and women.
These slippers were sometimes called *carpet slippers.*

Shoes for Fun and Sports

Shoes kept changing in style and shape.

Highly decorated shoes were worn for dancing and parties.

These shoes were very popular with men. They are called *brogues*. Some movie stars wore these shoes, too!

Look at the early sports shoes in this photograph.
They were worn by people playing tennis.

Look at these early
mountain-climbing boots.
The soles had nails in
them to help the climber
cling to the mountain.

Modern Shoes

Look how far the shoe has traveled!

People are still wearing high heels, just like they did hundreds and hundreds of years ago.

And shoes for parties and dances are still very beautiful.

Sandals are still good to wear when it's very hot. They help keep our feet cool.

Today, moccasins look very different. *Loafers* are shoes that look like moccasins, too.

Look at these modern mountain-climbing boots. They have metal spikes attached to their soles.

Sports shoes are comfortable, stylish, and very, very popular.

Look at these shoes!

They look like sports shoes, but people wear them to be fashionable, not to play sports.

Stepping Through Time

Prehistoric

1250 BC

100 AD

700 AD

1000 AD

1500
AD

1800
AD

1900
AD

Present

Index